This book belongs to

A Read-Aloud Storybook

Adapted by Lisa Ann Marsoli
Illustrated by the Disney Storybook Artists
Designed by Disney Publishing's Global Design Group

Random House New York

 Published in the United States by Random House Children's Books, a division of Random House, Inc., New York, and simultaneously in Canada by Random House of Canada Limited, Toronto, in conjunction with Disney Enterprises, Inc. RANDOM HOUSE and colophon are registered trademarks of Random House, Inc.
Library of Congress Control Number: 2004117462 ISBN 0-7364-2329-X

www.randomhouse.com/kids/disney

Printed in the United States of America

10 9 8 7 6 5 4 3 2 1

A Chicken with a Past

DONG! *DONG! DONG! DONG!*

"Emergency!" Chicken Little yelled, pulling the bell rope at the school tower as hard as he could. "Run for your lives!"

Down below, everyone in town heard the big bell ring out over Oakey Oaks. They dashed into the streets, screaming.

"The sky is falling!" shouted Chicken Little. "The sky is falling!"

Soon everyone was following Chicken Little to the old oak tree, where he said the sky had fallen and actually hit him on his head!

But there was no piece of sky on the ground. Everyone stared at Chicken Little, waiting for an explanation.

Finally, Chicken Little's dad, Buck, took charge. "It's okay, everyone," he called out. "It was just an acorn that hit my son."

Chicken Little hung his head in shame. Not even his father believed him.

A year later, the citizens of Oakey Oaks still remembered Chicken Little as "that crazy little chicken." They were even making a movie about his terrible mistake.

But Chicken Little had a plan. "One moment destroyed my life, right?" he said to his dad. "So I figure all I need is a second great moment to erase the previous first moment. Huh? What do you think?"

Buck sighed. "Don't call attention to yourself," he told his son, dropping him off at the bus stop. "Lie low."

Soon the school bus arrived, and all the kids raced to the doors. Tiny Chicken Little was knocked down and left lying on the ground as the bus pulled away.

Plucky guy that he was, he picked himself up and ran after the bus. He might have caught it, too, if the school bully, Foxy Loxy, hadn't dropped a bag of acorns out the window. Chicken Little slipped and slid until he landed with a THUD.

Determined to make it to school on time, Chicken Little raced across the street . . . and got stuck on a wad of gum.

As the morning traffic headed right toward him, Chicken Little pulled a lollipop out of his pocket, licked it, then stuck it to the back of a passing car. The car pulled him free just in time. Chicken Little felt the thrill of success. He also felt oddly chilly. He had lost his pants!

Hiding all the way, Chicken Little raced to school in his underpants. He wouldn't be able to enter through the front door, so he bought a soda from a nearby machine, shook it up, and launched himself through an open window. Once at his locker, he folded a page of his math notebook into a pair of paper pants. Now he was finally ready to face the day!

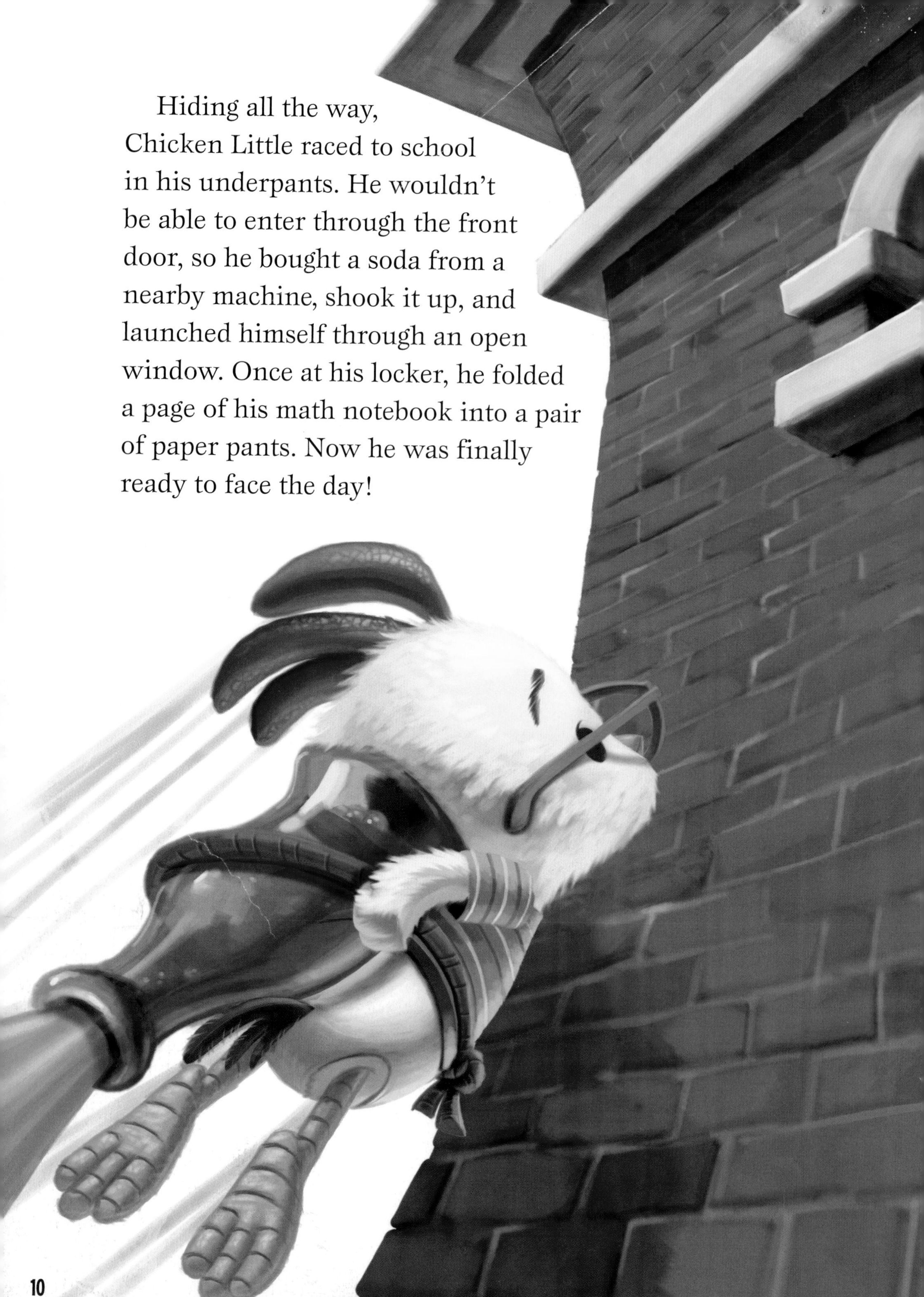

Chicken Little caught up with his friends Runt, Abby, and Fish in gym class. They were playing a furious game of dodgeball. Chicken Little told Abby his plan to make everyone forget the "sky is falling" incident by doing something great.

Just then, Chicken Little watched in horror as Foxy Loxy slammed a ball at Abby's face.

"That does it!" declared Chicken Little, defending his duck friend from the fox bully. "We were in a time-out, Foxy. Prepare to hurt!"

But Foxy Loxy's sidekick, Goosey Loosey, grabbed Chicken Little and flung him against the window. As he slid down, Chicken Little accidentally grabbed the fire alarm! The siren went off, and so did the overhead sprinklers.

Athlete of the Year
Buck Cluck
BUCK CLUCK LEADS ACORNS TO VICTORY
BUCK "ACE" CLUCK WINS BIG GAME
Buck Cluck

That afternoon, the principal gave Buck an earful behind closed doors. Chicken Little waited on the bench outside. He felt awful. He had disappointed his father again. To make matters worse, the display case in the hall was still filled with trophies from Buck's days as a star baseball player. Buck had never been a loser.

Suddenly, Chicken Little got an idea! He could join the baseball team. Maybe things would turn around and everyone would forget about his big mistake once and for all.

Chicken Little's plan seemed doomed from the start. Being the tiniest player on the Oakey Oaks Acorns baseball team, he always sat on the bench.

Then, in the final game against the Spud Valley Taters, Chicken Little was miraculously called to the plate.

"I won't embarrass you, Dad," Chicken Little whispered as he looked into the stands. "Not this time."

After two strikes, Chicken Little prepared for the third pitch. "Today is a new day," he told himself as he swung the bat with all his might.

To everyone's surprise, he got a hit! Chicken Little's legs pumped furiously as he ran around the bases. But when the pint-sized player slid into home plate, he was called out. The crowd groaned . . . until the announcer shouted, "Wait!"

The umpire dusted away the mound of dirt that covered Chicken Little's foot. "Safe! The runner is safe!"

The Acorns had won! Chicken Little was the new town hero!

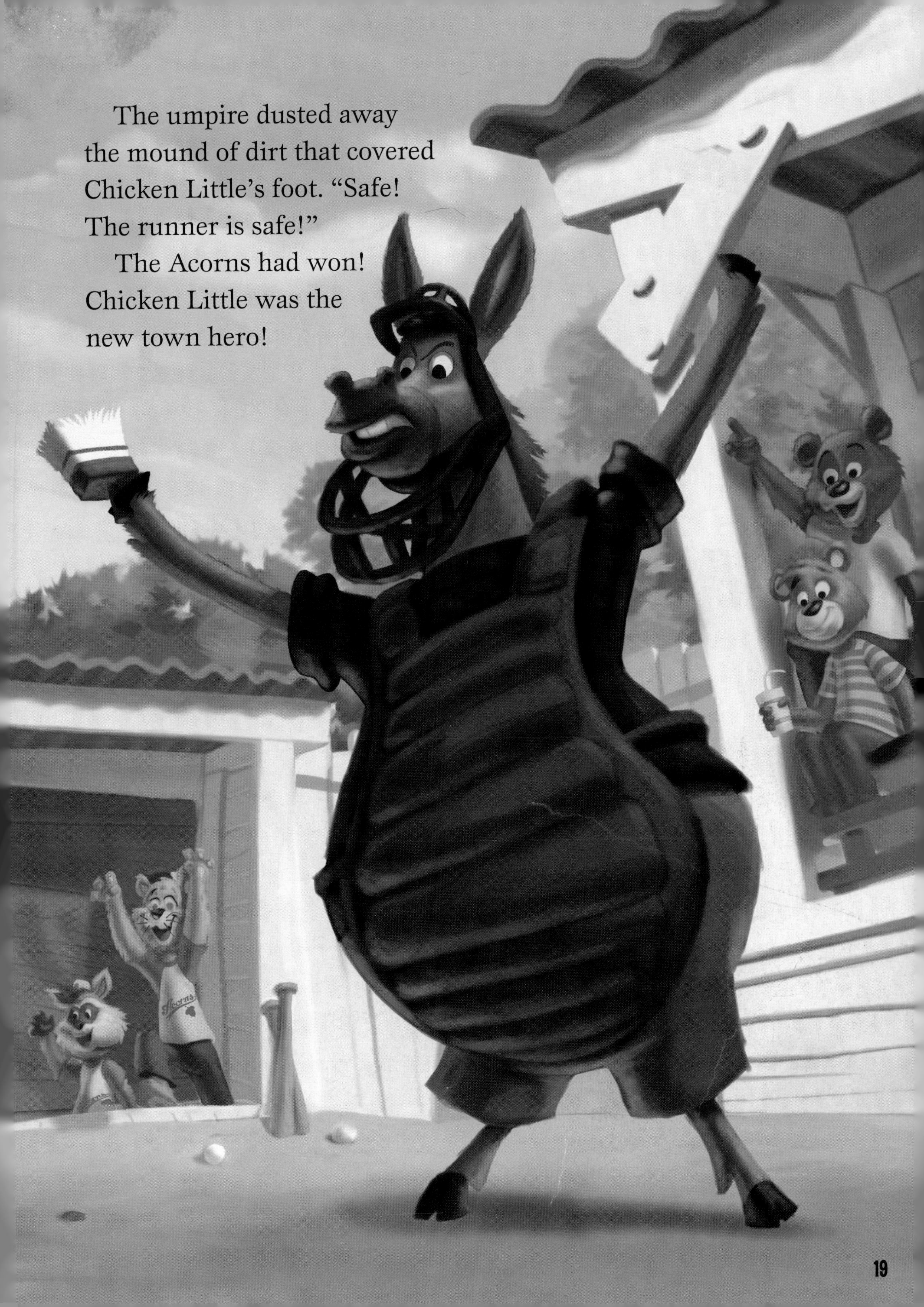

Back at home, Buck and his son had a great time reliving Chicken Little's winning home run.

"I guess that puts the whole 'sky is falling' incident behind us once and for all, eh, kiddo?" asked Buck.

"You bet, Dad," Chicken Little answered happily. He felt sure they were finally on the way to the close relationship he had been longing for.

The Sky Falls Again

After Buck went downstairs, Chicken Little gazed out his window. Suddenly, one star fell out of the sky and straight through Chicken Little's window! However, it wasn't a star at all, but a strange panel that changed colors. It looked exactly like the piece of sky that had fallen on him one year earlier.

Chicken Little gasped. "No. It's impossible!"

Chicken Little telephoned his friends Abby, Runt, and Fish. They stopped their karaoke and raced over to help. Abby took one look at the panel and said, "Okay. Let me guess. You haven't told your dad yet."

"Abby, please," Chicken Little begged. "This is exactly what fell on me the first time! There's no way I'm bringing this up again with him."

Meanwhile, the panel floated off the ground and zoomed out the window—with Fish on top of it!

ACORNS

Chicken Little, Abby, and Runt raced outside to find Fish. They couldn't see their friend. Instead, they saw a glowing light stick up in the sky—the same light stick Fish had been holding during karaoke earlier that night. Fish was invisible, but his light stick wasn't! Chicken Little and Abby chased after the zooming light as fast as they could. Runt did his best to keep up.

The chase led the friends to the baseball stadium. Suddenly, a fierce cyclone swirled around them. They ran to the safety of the dugout just in time to see a spaceship! The strange ship's hatch opened, and two scary-looking aliens with long tentacles climbed out.

"Poor Fish," wailed Runt. "He's gone! Gone, man."

But then, miraculously, Fish appeared, waving from the top of the ship!

The two aliens floated across the ball field and disappeared into the night.

The frightened friends climbed into the spaceship to rescue Fish. As they made their way along a dark, creepy corridor, Chicken Little stopped to examine a furry orange creature floating in a blue light. The fascinated chicken winked, and the furry thing winked back! As Chicken Little hurried onward, he did not notice that the little creature was following him!

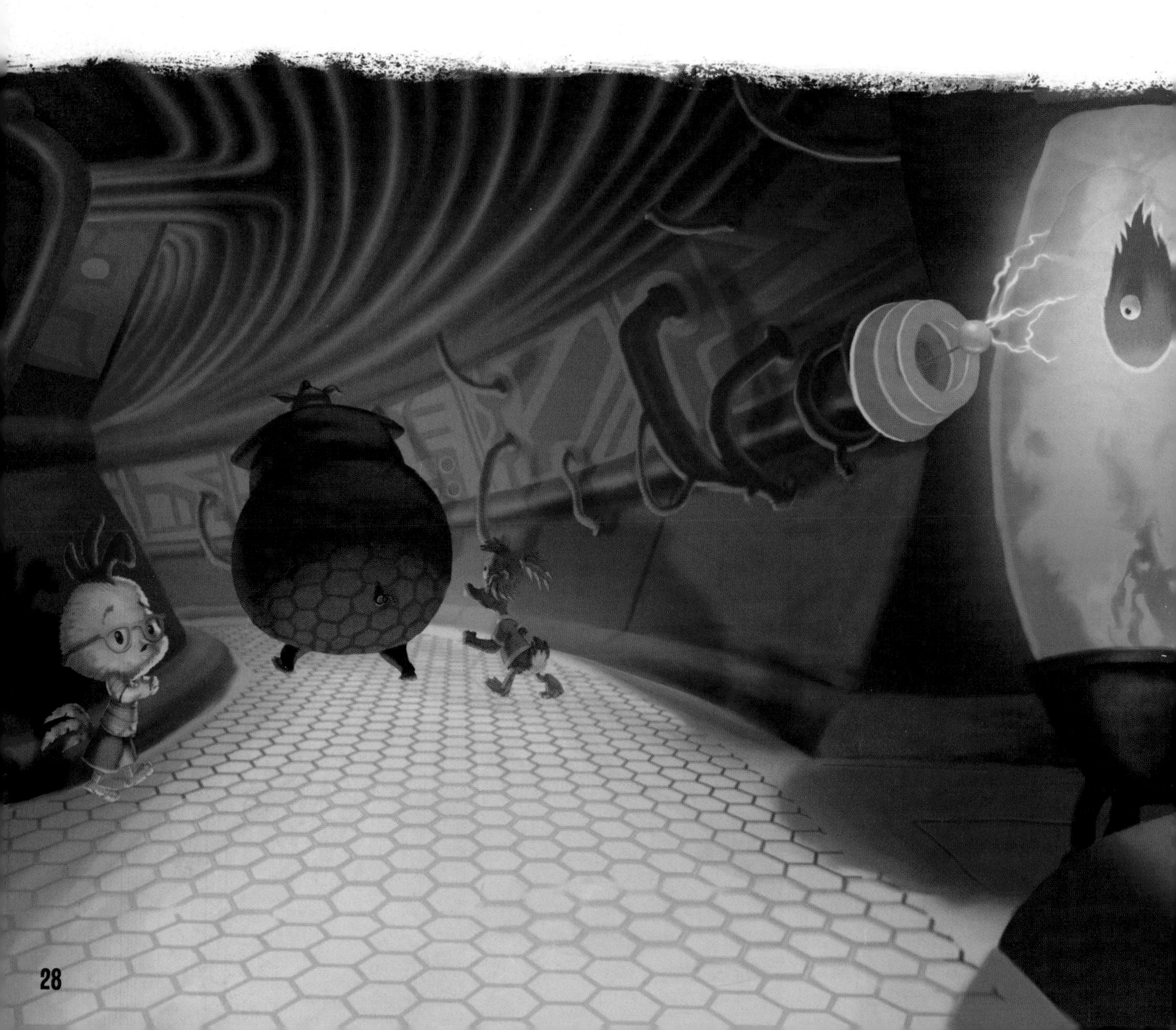

The three friends continued their search, nervously calling Fish's name. Then Chicken Little spotted a screen of slime—with Fish's skeleton in it! Runt nearly fainted. To their enormous relief, Fish, looking like his old self, popped out from behind the screen.

"Did they hurt you?" Abby asked, knocking on Fish's helmet.

"Don't tap the glass," Chicken Little told her. "They hate it when you do that."

Meanwhile, Runt had made a horrifying discovery. It was a glowing map of a trail of planets, each one crossed out with a big red X. And the next planet on the trail was Earth! The aliens' attack plan was clear.

"We're next!" Chicken Little gulped.

The reunited friends ran back toward the hatch as fast as they could. Unfortunately, the aliens had returned!

The two aliens looked at the empty blue light shaft where the furry orange creature had been. Then they began to chase Chicken Little and his friends!

Chicken Little, Runt, Abby, and Fish dashed to the hatch with the aliens close behind. They made it out just ahead of the aliens and headed toward the woods as fast as they could.

After the four friends had made their way through the trees, they tripped and rolled down a steep hill into a cornfield. They hid, terrified, as the aliens searched the field. Suddenly, the aliens' tentacles sprouted spinning blades, cutting down every cornstalk in sight. Chicken Little and the others darted through the plants, trying desperately to escape.

Nobody saw the little orange creature watching them.

“We’ve got to ring the school bell to warn everyone!” said Abby.

Chicken Little and his friends ran frantically toward the school, but the doors were locked. Thinking quickly, Chicken Little used his fizzy soda trick to launch himself to the bell tower. Down below, the aliens had cornered Runt, Abby, and Fish. There was no time to lose!

Chicken Little was about to pull the rope when memories of the last time he had rung the bell came rushing back to him. He knew that he risked embarrassing his father and becoming the laughingstock of the town all over again. But if he didn't ring the bell, he was risking the lives of his friends—and everyone else in Oakey Oaks.

So Chicken Little bravely sounded the alarm.

By the time the townsfolk arrived, the aliens had already fled back to the cornfield. Chicken Little urged the crowd to hurry with him to the baseball stadium, where the spaceship had landed.

But just before they went through the gates, the mayor made everyone halt. He had found a penny and wanted to pick it up.

When everyone finally made it to the stadium, the spaceship had disappeared.

"I know this looks bad," Chicken Little explained, "but there's an invisible spaceship right there!" Chicken Little began throwing rocks in the air, trying to hit the ship to prove it was there. Hitting nothing, the rocks fell to the ground one by one. "You see, there are these cloaking panels on the bottom that make it disappear. And I know this because one fell out of the sky and hit me on the head."

“It’s the acorn thing all over again,” someone shouted.

“No, wait! There *were* aliens!” insisted Abby.

“They had three big red eyes, and claws, and hooks and tentacles,” added Runt.

“I’m telling the truth!” cried Chicken Little. “Dad! I’m not making this up! You’ve got to believe me this time!”

But Buck didn't believe him.

"I can't tell you how embarrassed I am, folks." Buck managed an awkward smile as he spoke to the angry crowd. "I'm really sorry about this, everyone."

Buck took one last look at his son and then walked away.

Chicken Little had never felt so alone.

Meanwhile, the fuzzy orange creature from the spaceship was hiding nearby. It watched as the alien craft grew smaller and smaller in the sky overhead. Left behind on a strange planet, it felt just as alone as Chicken Little did. The little creature decided to follow the only earthling it recognized. . . .

Family Matters

The next day, Oakey Oaks was still not back to normal. Buck spent hours answering phone calls, e-mails, and even sky-written messages—each one complaining about the total chaos Chicken Little had caused . . . again.

But the chaos was just beginning. In the backyard, Chicken Little's friends were trying to cheer him up when suddenly the furry orange creature appeared! He seemed upset, but nobody could understand what he was saying—except Fish.

As the alien babbled and blubbered, Fish translated for his friends. They learned that the furry creature was an alien child who had been accidentally left behind by his parents.

AKS
CHEESE
fine china

Suddenly, a fleet of spaceships appeared over the town of Oakey Oaks. The aliens thought that Chicken Little had kidnapped the alien child!

Buck raced to find his son. "You were right—alien invasion," Buck said when he found Chicken Little. "I see that now."

Chicken Little wanted to explain that it was a rescue, not an invasion—but he didn't think his dad would believe him. Instead, he ran off with his friends to help the little alien, who was running desperately toward the spaceships.

Buck Cluck caught up with his son in the movie theater. It was time for a much-needed heart-to-heart talk.

"You've been ashamed of me since the acorn thing happened!" Chicken Little blurted out.

Buck felt terrible for not believing in his son. It was time for a change. "You need to know that I love you, no matter what."

Then Buck leaned down and hugged his son. It was all Chicken Little had ever wanted.

"Let's go!" Abby shouted, pointing outside at the attacking aliens.

"Okay, Dad," Chicken Little said, "now all we've got to do is return this helpless little kid."

The tiny alien appeared from behind the curtain. He leaped on top of Buck and began biting him!

"This orange bitey thing needs saving?" replied Buck doubtfully. "I've never heard of such a crazy . . . crazy, *wonderful* idea. Just tell me what you need me to do!"

"C'mon, Dad!" said Chicken Little, elated. "We've got a planet to save!"

Before they left the theater, a newly confident Chicken Little marched up to Abby. After planting a great big kiss on her bill, he announced, "By the way, I would like to say I have always found you extremely attractive!"

Buck and Chicken Little headed outside, carrying the little alien with them. All around them, aliens were zapping everything with laser beams.

"We surrender!" yelled Mayor Turkey Lurkey. "Here, take the key to the city!"

But the aliens wouldn't stop.

Buck and Chicken Little climbed with the little alien to the top of Town Hall. They tried to give the child back to his parents, hoping to end the battle. Unfortunately, they were beamed aboard the spaceship instead!

Three huge eyes appeared on a screen.
"WHY DID YOU TAKE OUR CHILD?" a deep voice boomed.
"You were the one that left him behind," Buck tried to explain.
The big voice interrupted him, "SILENCE! RELEASE THE CHILD!"
So Buck did exactly that.

Suddenly, the screen shut off and the alien child's parents—Tina and Mel—appeared. The parents weren't scary-looking at all without their space suits on. And they were much friendlier after their child explained what had really happened!

OAKUS OAKUM

Grateful for the return of the child, the aliens quickly repaired the damage to the town. “If it hadn’t been for your son there, we might have vaporized the whole planet,” Mel told Buck. Then he explained why they had stopped on Earth in the first place—to pick acorns! Acorns were considered a special treat on Mel’s planet.

And so Chicken Little became the town's hero . . . again.

One year later, the townsfolk of Oakey Oaks crowded into the local theater to see *Chicken Little: The True Story*.

"Though at times it may feel like the sky is falling around you—never give up," the actor playing Chicken Little said heroically. "For every day is a new day!"

The audience cheered at the end of the movie. Then they turned and directed their applause at Buck and Chicken Little.

Chicken Little looked at his dad and smiled. It felt great being a hero—but it felt even better knowing that his dad would always be there for him. No matter what.